To our Duckie Dimples, Katie,
who is always ready to interpret the rules her own way
–A. L.

To my dearest cousin Mathilde, the coolest pet lover I could ever know
–É. C.

STERLING CHILDREN'S BOOKS
New York

An Imprint of Sterling Publishing Co., Inc.
1166 Avenue of the Americas
New York, NY 10036

Text © 2018 Alexandria LaFaye
Illustrations © 2018 Églantine Ceulemans

ISBN 978-1-4549-2698-6

Distributed in Canada by Sterling Publishing Co., Inc.
c/o Canadian Manda Group, 664 Annette Street
Toronto, Ontario M6S 2C8, Canada
Distributed in the United Kingdom by GMC Distribution Services
Castle Place, 166 High Street, Lewes, East Sussex BN7 1XU, England
Distributed in Australia by NewSouth Books
45 Beach Street, Coogee, NSW 2034, Australia

For information about custom editions, special sales, and premium and corporate purchases,
please contact Sterling Special Sales at 800-805-5489 or specialsales@sterlingpublishing.com.

Manufactured in Canada

Lot #:
2 4 6 8 10 9 7 5 3 1
06/18

sterlingpublishing.com

Jacket and interior design by Ryan Thomann
The artwork in this book was created with multiple media : pencils, indian ink, colorex inks, and Adobe Photoshop.

No Frogs in School

by A. LaFaye   illustrated by Églantine Ceulemans

STERLING CHILDREN'S BOOKS
New York

Bartholomew Botts loved pets.

Hoppy pets, hairy pets, and scaly pets. He loved them all so much that he couldn't go to school without one.

On Monday, Bartholomew chose
Ferdinand the frog, because he was
new to the family.

Bartholomew plopped him in his
cool pink lunchbox.

During art, Mr. Patanoose taught them how mixing colors made new colors. Bartholomew wondered what made frogs different colors.

Just when Bartholomew was about to ask, Ferdinand jumped into Lacey's finger paints.

Bartholomew grabbed
for Ferdinand, but
he slip-hopped away.

On Tuesday, Sigfried the salamander looked lonely.

He wasn't a frog, so Bartholomew figured Mr. Patanoose wouldn't mind. He slipped Sigfried into his pocket.

When Bartholomew showed him to Sanford,
Sigfried skittered up Sanford's sleeve.

Sanford **sha- sha- shoomed** to get him out.

Bartholomew scrambled to catch the salamander.
Sigfried scampered onto a desk, then scurried to the floor.

The other kids started to scream and scramble.

Sigfried got nervous.

He went **WOO-WOO** on Mr. Patanoose's shoe.

$3+4=7$

WINTER SPRI

Mr. Patanoose shared a new rule.

"No salamanders in school. No frogs, toads, or tadpoles. Nothing born in the water that grows up to live on land. Keep your amphibians at home!"

On Wednesday, Horace the hamster didn't want to go back in his house. He wasn't an amphibian, so Bartholomew put Horace in his bag. Horace hated pockets.

Mr. Patanoose liked pockets. He wanted to see inside every one Bartholomew had.

"See how popular pockets are?" Bartholomew told Horace. But he didn't hear a word. The hamster had wandered off.

"Time to check our seedlings!" said Mr. Patanoose.

Bartholomew loved gardening, so he got to the planting box first.

Actually, Horace got there first.

He squealed and squirmed and shimmied between the seedlings.

Everyone got in on the act, grabbing and shouting and laughing.

Horace got so scared, he scurried
back to Bartholomew's pocket!

STRAWBERRY

Mr. Patanoose added a new rule.

"No hamsters. No rats.
No squirrels. No rodents
in school!"

On Thursday, Sylvia the snake snuggled around Bartholomew's hand. She wasn't an amphibian or a rodent, so Bartholomew said he'd slip her into school with him.

Mr. Patanoose asked
Bartholomew to turn
his bag inside out.
Bartholomew said he could
do the same thing with
his top lip. Mr. Patanoose
didn't want to see it.

Mr. Patanoose talked
to the class about full
sentences and periods.
Carlos leaned over to
Bartholomew and asked,
"Can you show me the
lip thing?"

Bartholomew did.
Carlos laughed.

Bartholomew took Sylvia out of her box to show Carlos that snakes have a notch in their lips for their tongue to go through.

But Fatima screamed and scared Sylvia. She slithered right up the wall.

"Wow!" Raul pointed.
"Does it bite?"

Bartholomew said,
"No, she snuggles."

Mr. Patanoose came over with dust in his hair and a snake in his hand. He didn't look happy, and he had a new rule. This one was a doozie:

"No snakes in school. No turtles. No lizards. No cold-blooded animals with scales. No reptiles!"

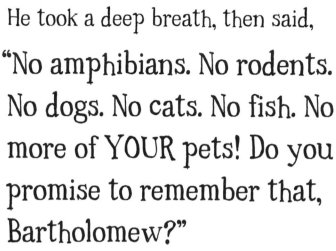

He took a deep breath, then said,

"No amphibians. No rodents. No dogs. No cats. No fish. No more of YOUR pets! Do you promise to remember that, Bartholomew?"

"Yes, Mr. Patanoose." Bartholomew was good at following the rules.

Mr. Patanoose said, "Tomorrow, we'll start the day with show and tell."

"Can we bring anything?" asked Fatima.

"Yes, anything."
Mr. Patanoose stared at Bartholomew. "But no more of YOUR pets."

On Friday, Bartholomew sat on his bed with Rivka, the rabbit, in his lap.

Bartholomew thought she'd enjoy going to school and meeting all of the kids.

Too bad about Mr. Patanoose's rules. Rivka wasn't an amphibian or a rodent, but she was his pet. Then he had an idea. A hoppy, happy, can't-wait-for-it-to-happen idea.

He smiled about it all the way to school.

Mr. Patanoose didn't look so happy when Bartholomew came into the classroom. "What is that?"

"It's Rivka. And she's not MY pet. She's EVERYONE'S pet."

And that's how Rivka came to live in Mr. Patanoose's classroom. And no one was happier than Bartholomew, because Bartholomew Botts loved pets. Hoppy pets, hairy pets, scaly pets, and classroom ones, too.